THE RED FEATHER LADIES GET THEIR MAN was first produced by the Sun City Players in Sun City, California on Novermber 1, 2008. The performance was directed by Maxine Holmgren. The cast was as follows:

BETTY. . . . . Betty Jo Adney

ALICE . . . . Faye Hartline

LOUISE . . . . Pat Mogge

JANE . . . . .Donna Ogier

BARBARA . . . . .Donna Blair

CHARLENE . . . . C. Susan Carreiro

ROSEANN . . . . .Marcia Stroope

CHARACTERS

BETTY – The Prime Plume of the Red Feather Ladies Investment Club. She is a retired attorney. She is suspicious of everything and everyone.

LOUISE – A fun loving, adventurous member of the Red Feather group. A former cheer leader, she is always cheerful. Tends to be loud and brash.

CHARLENE – A shy, quiet, studious member of the group. She is not very well coordinated and is prone to dropping things, knocking things over and bumping into things.

BARBARA – A pill popping hypochondriac. She always has health problems but looks the picture of health and never misses a meeting.

JANE – A sophisticated socialite. Her position in society is very important to her. She is very dramatic and demonstrative in her manner of speech.

ROSEANN – A sweet, naïve member of the Red Feather Investment Club. She is from the South, and speaks with a Southern drawl.

(NOTE: All of these characters wear something with a large red feather. It could be on a hat, purse, boa or any accessory.)

WAITRESS – Wears typical waitress outfit. She is not too bright.

SETTING

The play takes place in The Fancy Frills tea room. There is a door to the outside on stage right, a door to the kitchen on stage left. A long table and chairs are center stage, smaller tables set for tea guests are also on stage. The room should be decorated as a typical tea room, very feminine. There are pretty floral pictures and arrangements on the walls. A large easel is on one side of the stage or on the apron of the stage. A poster with the tea room name sits on it. This should also be decorated with flowers. A clock is on the wall.

The Red Feather Ladies Get Their Man

A Sequel to
Revenge of the Red Feather Ladies

by Maxine Holmgren

Baker's Plays
7611 Sunset Blvd.
Los Angeles, CA 90042
bakersplays.com

(*SETTING: Fancy Frills Tea Room*)

(***AT RISE:*** *It is mid-day.* **BETTY** *is seated at the head of a table set for six. She is studying a menu, as she waits impatiently for others. She taps her fingers, looks at watch, etc.*)

WAITRESS. (*Enters from kitchen, order pad in hand. Approaches* **BETTY**. *Does not look at her, but reads from order pad.*) Hello, my name is Alice. I'll be your server today. Are you ready to order?

BETTY. I'm waiting for five others. They're late as usual.

WAITRESS. (*confused*) So – you're not ready to order?

BETTY. On the contrary. I am perfectly ready to order. I know exactly what I want, but I prefer to wait for my five tardy friends before I order.

WAITRESS. (*doesn't know what to do*) Oh. Should I come back?

BETTY. (*sarcastically*) No, I want you to sit down and tell me the story of your life.

(*loudly*)

Of course, I want you to come back!

WAITRESS. Uh, when should I come back?

BETTY. When you see five other people here, that's when.

WAITRESS. (*repeats and writes in her pad as she begin to exit*) Come back when there are five people at table.

BETTY. No! Five other others plus myself. That makes six.

WAITRESS. (*erases from notepad*) Six. Come back when there are six at the table.

BETTY. Yes.

WAITRESS. I'll come back when there are six. (*exits*)

LOUISE. (*Enters. Sits next to* **BETTY**.*) Hi, Betty. Whew, I thought for sure I was gonna be late, but here I am, right on time.

BETTY. The monthly meeting of the Red Feather Ladies' Investment Club was supposed to start *(looks at her watch)* five minutes ago, but as usual, most of the members are late. We'll just have to wait for the rest to arrive.

LOUISE. I thought it was a great idea having the meeting at this tea room. I like tea and they don't serve it down at Barney's Grill, where I usually have lunch.

JANE. *(Enters, making a dramatic entrance. Pauses at door, looks around room. Walks slowly as if on parade to table and sits next to **LOUISE**.)* Hello, darlings. Sorry to be a wee bit tardy. I had to tear myself away from the Committee meeting for the Cotillion Ball. They value my input so much, they just wouldn't let me leave until I'd answered all their questions.

LOUISE. What's a cotillion ball? I've heard of a soccer ball and a rugby ball, but I ain't ever heard of a cotillion ball.

JANE. It's not a ball used in sports, my dear. It's a formal evening dinner dance for debutants. Where is the waitress? I'd like some tea, or at least water.

BETTY. *(calling)* Waitress! Oh, waitress!

BARBARA. *(Enters. Walks with difficulty, using walker or cane.)* Hello, girls. Oh, my arthritis is just terrible today. I wasn't sure I could even come today, but I didn't want to miss our meeting. I think it's important we stick together. *(sits next to **JANE**)*

JANE. Yes, I can hardly wait to get an update.

LOUISE. Just the thought of that two-timer makes my blood boil.

BETTY. *(calling)* Waitress! Where did she go?

WAITRESS. *(enters with hesitation)* Do you want me to come back now? There aren't six of you yet.

BETTY. Well, come back anyway. We'd like some water or tea.

WAITRESS. Water or tea?

BETTY. Yes.

WAITRESS. *(confused)* Well, water or tea?

BETTY. Oh, good grief! Just bring us some water.

JANE. With lemon, please.

BARBARA. No lemon for me. All that acid would upset my stomach.

WAITRESS. I better write that down.

(exits)

(CHARLENE & ROSEANN *enter together.* **CHARLENE** *carries books, water bottle, purse, etc.)*

CHARLENE. It's a good thing you came along just when you did, Roseann. I don't know how I would have been able to open the door with everything I was carrying. Thank you!

(drops book)

ROSEANN. That's alright, sweetie. Let me help you. Hello, everyone.

(Pulls out chair for **CHARLENE** *at end of table.* **ROSE-ANN** *sits next to* **BARBARA.** *)*

CHARLENE. *(plopping down in chair, knocking things over as she does so)* I can't wait to hear how everyone turned out.

(WAITRESS *returns with waters for all. Sees* **ROSEANN** *and* **CHARLENE,** *and counts six. Exits.)*

BETTY. Waitress! Now where did she go?

LOUISE. Is that the same dumb waitress we had last time we were here?

BETTY. Yes, so let's not confuse her any more than she already is. Let's just all order the same thing.

BARBARA. I knew I should have brought my protein bars. I have to be very careful what I eat, you know. I better take some antacid right now.

WAITRESS. *(enters, speaks to everyone, hands out menus)* I'll come back now. Hello. My name is Alice. I'll be your server today.

BETTY. We'll all have the same thing. Just a Queen's tea for everyone. Separate checks, please.

WAITRESS. You all want the Queen's tea? I don't think we can do that. It's not enough for six people, and how could I put it on separate checks? I'd have to divide the price by six, and what would I do about the tax?

BETTY. *(exasperated)* No! No! I mean that each one of us wants one order of the Queen's tea. That's a total of six Queen's teas.

WAITRESS. Oh, that's much better. So you were only joking when you said you wanted a Queens tea for six. That's funny!

LOUISE. Yeah, she's a laugh a minute.

*(***WAITRESS*** exits.)*

BETTY. Well, ladies, I'm glad you could all attend this meeting.

JANE. I certainly hope it's a better meeting than the last one.

CHARLENE. Me, too. I cried through most of the last meeting.

ROSEANN. What we all learned at the last meeting was hard on all of us.

BARBARA. It nearly did me in. I had to take three tranquilizers and four blood pressure pills.

LOUISE. Yeah. We all thought we had good news to share, each one of us was gonna get married.

JANE. Yes, until we discovered we were all engaged to the same man!

LOUISE. Yeah, the dirty rat. He used a different name with each one of us and saw each one on a different night of the week. My night was Mondays. Mondays with Willy.

CHARLENE. Tuesdays were my big news days, with Billy.

BARBARA. I don't know how he kept it all straight. William only dated me on Wednesdays.

JANE. Willard always took me out to dinner on Thursdays.

ROSEANN. Fridays were my big night with Wilson.

BETTY. I had Bill all to myself – on Saturdays. *(takes out large picture, looks at it wistfully, places face down on table)*

ALL TOGETHER. But never on Sundays.

JANE. It's just a good thing you discovered what that roving Romeo was up too, Betty. You were the one that got suspicious, and hired a detective to secretly take his picture.

BETTY. I may be retired from law practice, but those years of practicing law have left me suspicious of everyone. It's a good thing I still have lots of friends in the justice field. And we all want justice, right girls?

ROSEANN. When you showed us the picture of your fiancé – and it turned out it was the same man that each one of us was engaged too – I nearly fainted!

CHARLENE. I still can't believe it. My Billy was so sweet, so kind, so handsome. I know I was terribly angry at first-

BARBARA. What do you mean – at first? Aren't you still angry? Just the thought of what he did to us all gives me a headache. In fact, I should probably use some nose spray before I get another sinus headache.

JANE. If I remember right, Barbara is correct. You were so angry with him, you were going to do something through the computer to get into his bank account for revenge.

CHARLENE. *(sniffling as she explains)* Well, I got to thinking things over. I thought about all the nice things he did, and the way he whispered my name and stroked my hair when he explained why he couldn't pay the rent on the apartment he leased from me. I just couldn't evict him.

BETTY. What about emptying his on-line bank account and maxing out his credit card like you said you were going to do.

CHARLENE. But if I did that, how could he send money to all those missionaries in Africa? He supported three orphanages, one hospital, and six schools in Africa. I just know he wouldn't make up a story like that. He has such honest eyes.

BARBARA. *(dreaming)* He did have lovely eyes.

(WAITRESS enters and serves scones and tea.)

CHARLENE. I asked him why he could only see me on Tuesdays, and he had a perfectly good explanation.

LOUISE. This I gotta hear.

CHARLENE. He explained that he worked with the homeless on Mondays, and on Wed. he visited a sick friend.

BARBARA. Is that what he called our dates? Visits with a sick friend? I need another pain pill!

CHARLENE. Then on Thursdays, he worked on fund raisers for various charities. He said he often had to escort elderly dowagers to society events to raise money for the sick and poor.

JANE. *(insulted)* Elderly dowager! That's what he said about being with me? The nerve of that man!

CHARLENE. Friday night was his bowling night with his redneck friend. He said he'd be glad to take me bowling, but he didn't think I'd like his friend. Said he had a drinking problem and that he was trying to help him overcome it.

BETTY. I can't wait to hear his excuse for Saturday.

CHARLENE. Well, on Saturday night he had to read several chapters of the Bible and prepare for the Sunday School class he taught. You see, all perfectly sound reasons.

JANE. What about the picture? It was a picture of the man we were all engaged to.

CHARLENE. It must be someone that looks like him. He said he's always being mistaken for someone else.

BETTY. Charlene, do you mean to tell us that you believe everything he said? You're not angry anymore?

CHARLENE. Yes. I mean No. Yes, I believe him. No, I'm not angry. I'm in love with him, and we're still going to be married.

JANE. But, surely, you're not going to go to Hawaii as planned?

CHARLENE. Yes, I am. But I reminded him I didn't like to go sailing on the ocean. You girls had me thinking he might try to throw me overboard to collect the life insurance. So he said he'd take me deep sea fishing instead, and I could feed the fish. Doesn't that sound like fun?

ROSEANN. We've got to stop this double crosser before someone gets hurt. Louise, didn't you have a plan to take care of the scoundrel?

BARBARA. If I remember right, you said you had a cousin that was in the Mafia!

JANE. Quite shocking!

WAITRESS. *(enters, takes away scones before they finish eating them)* Oh, I've been to Mafia on the coast. It's a lovely place.

BETTY. Just serve the food.

LOUISE. As I was saying, about my cousin Nick. I don't see him very often; we travel in different circles, if you know what I mean. But a long time ago, when we were just kids, I helped him out of a little jam he was in. He was so grateful that I never squealed to his Ma about it, that he said if I ever, ever needed help, I just give him a call.

ROSEANN. That's so sweet. Childhood promises. So, you called him?

LOUISE. Well, I tried to. Like I said, I don't see him very often these days. In fact, we kind of fell out of touch with each other. I'd heard he'd been in trouble with the police more than once. The phone number I had for him was disconnected. I finally got in touch with his Ma, and she told me the news.

ROSEANN. I bet he had reformed and was a preacher now!

LOUISE. Not quite. It seems he's staying at an all expense paid Big House as a guest of the government.

CHARLENE. Really? Did he win the lotto or something?

BETTY. I think she means something entirely different, Charlene.

ROSEANN. Big house? You mean he's in prison? Oh, dear.

LOUISE. Exactly. So, I went to see him on visiting day. Whew, what an ordeal just to get to say hello. It took an hour just to get through security, and then I had to talk to him through a dirty glass window.

JANE. How disgusting. So he was no help to you at all, was he?

LOUISE. Actually, Nick was true to his word. I told Nick all about the two timing gigolo that conned us all, and he was real sorry he couldn't take care of him hisself. But he had a friend that could do it for me, he said. He gave me a phone number to call, but he made me promise not to tell his Ma about it. The hitman's name was Pat, so I called as soon as I got home.

(**WAITRESS** *enters, serves main course.*)

BARBARA. It's so drafty in here. Isn't anyone else cold? Waitress, can you please turn up the heat?

(puts on sweater) Go on, Louise, I'm listening.

LOUISE. Well, when I called I got an answering machine. So I left a message, saying Nick sent me, and I had a job for him. I said if you're interested, meet me at the Daily Grind coffee shop the next morning at 10. I said I'd be wearing a large red feather in my hat so he'd recognize me.

BETTY. The very next morning! You didn't waste any time, did you?

LOUISE. You're darn right! I was mad, remember? So, I went to the coffee shop, and after a few minutes, a good looking gal saunters over and says to me, "So, how's Nick?" I nearly fell off my chair. Turns out Pat ain't a man at all, it's a woman. A hit woman. So, I tell her all about Willy, and all the aliases he used with us, and how we wanted to get even. We worked out all the details, and she said she'd be in touch.

JANE. *(shocked)* Oh, good heavens! She didn't try to murder him, did she?

LOUISE. Wait till you hear what happened. After I didn't hear nothing for a few weeks, I called her up again. She said she was working on the case. She was getting to know his habits, she said, so she could plan out the hit. She had been following him… She had pictures she took of him working out at the gym, and at a restaurant, and at the beach. Said she had to get to know him better so she could arrange the perfect place to stage the uh, accident.

BETTY. That's a strange way of doing it. What happened next?

LOUISE. Another couple of weeks went by, and I didn't hear anything from her. So, I called and set up another meeting. I'm getting impatient by now, you know. So, she comes in, and right away I can tell something's wrong. She's being real sweet and kind of coy, you know? Finally, she says she can't do the job after all. I ask why and she says "for personal reasons." I'm thinking maybe she's reformed or something. I question her some more and she finally admits that she's engaged. Now, get this! She's engaged to Willy! He's conned her, too!

(Everyone: exclamations of surprise)

But not to worry. Nick gets out of the pen in six months, and he'll take care of Willy himself. But don't tell his Ma.

CHARLENE. See? I told you! She must have met that guy that looks just like my fiancé.

BETTY. You're hopeless. Didn't anyone put a stop to this fraud?

BARBARA. Well, I had a great plan, but it didn't work out too well.

ROSEANN. Yes, I remember. You were going to switch some of your medications for some of his vitamins. That should have put him in the hospital and out of commission for awhile.

BARBARA. Yes, that was the plan alright. Just thinking about it gives me a headache.

(takes aspirin) If you remember, I was going to visit my pharmacist and get some extra potent diuretics and colon cleansers. Chuck, the pharmacist, and I have become good friends. He says I'm his very best customer. I told Chuck that I was very concerned about the mercury poisoning from the old fillings in my teeth, and that I wanted to cleanse my internal workings. He sold me a strong detoxification kit. He warned me to follow the directions carefully or there could be drastic side effects.

JANE. I can see where this is going.

BARBARA. So, when Wednesday night came along, I told William not to pick me up at my place because I was having the house tented for termites, and that I'd come to his apartment. When I got there, I told him I was feeling weak, and didn't want to go out for dinner, so he ordered Chinese food to be delivered.

LOUISE. Did you get it from Foo-Lling-Yu? I love that place!

BARBARA. *(ignoring her)* I was so nervous, I had to take a couple of tranquilizers. I mean, what if he caught me switching detox for vitamins? So, I decided it would be easier to just drop the detox powder in his drink.

LOUISE. Like a mickey-fin!

BARBARA. We were drinking sugar free, ice free, caffeine free cola when the food arrived, so when he went to the door, I dropped the detox powder in his drink.

ROSEANN. Good for you. Did he drink it all?

BARBARA. Well, I was so nervous and shaky that I dropped my egg roll and knocked over my drink trying to catch it.

BETTY. Oh, no. You poor thing.

BARBARA. So, he gave me his drink! I didn't know what to do, so I took another tranquilizer to calm me down and help me think straight. Then he got up to go get another drink for himself.

BETTY. Now you've got to switch glasses, right?

BARBARA. Right. He had put some ice in his drink, so I said Oh, I want ice, too – let's switch drinks, and I took his and gave him mine.

CHARLENE. I bet you were relieved you had the right glass.

BARBARA. Not for long. He said he'd just get himself another drink with ice. He came back to the table with his new drink and set it right next to the other two. I was getting a little dizzy, all those tranquilizers, I guess. But I was pretty sure I remembered which glass had the powder in it.

JANE. I hope you didn't have to eat Chinese food out of those awful Styrofoam containers. So uncouth.

BARBARA. Oh, no. He set a lovely table. But the table was crowded, so he moved the drinks to one side so he could serve the moo goo gai pan, and when he did, I thought the glasses got switched.

LOUISE. So, what did you do?

BARBARA. When he went out to the kitchen to get the fortune cookies I switched the glasses again. We ate the fortune cookies and finished the meal with a toast that everything in our relationship would come out all right.

BETTY. That was appropriate! How soon before he felt the results?

BARBARA. Oh, the result was almost immediate. I began to have terrible stomach pain, my left foot went numb and my face turned purple. William called 911 and I was rushed to the hospital. I went into a coma and was in critical condition for 36 hours.

ROSEANN. That's awful, Barbara. Did William come to see you?

BARBARA. Oh, yes. When they finally allowed me to have visitors, he was right there. He told me that he'd gone through my purse to find my insurance card, and found the detox kit from the pharmacy. He also found my diary and read all about my plans to take care of him. He said he never wanted to see me again, and demanded I return the engagement ring.

ROSEANN. What did you do?

BARBARA. I threw it at him. I was pretty weak, so it didn't go far. That's the last I saw of him – on his hands and knees looking for the ring under a chair. I think I passed out again after all that exertion. My, it's hot in here. *(fans herself)*

BETTY. I swear that man is like the cat with nine lives. So far, everyone has failed to get even with him! Jane, weren't you going to hire somebody to see to it that he left town and didn't cause you any embarrassment?

(WAITRESS *enters.)*

WAITRESS. (*clears main course*) I'll bring desert in a minute. I hope you don't want any more tea. It's a bother opening all those little tea bags with the string on them in order to put the tea in the pot. I don't know why they package them like that.

BARBARA. Waitress, it's so hot in here. Please turn up the air conditioning.

WAITRESS. I turned up the heat. I don't think I can run the air conditioning at the same time. But I'll try. I aim to please!

BETTY. Too bad she misses.

LOUISE. I hope he roughed him up good, if you know what I mean.

JANE. (*looks uncomfortable*) Well, it, uh, didn't go quite as I expected.

BETTY. Don't tell me you failed too!

JANE. No, I wouldn't call it a complete failure. I did hire someone. Remember, I said I would hire a security guard to guard the security of my social position. I didn't want it to be in the newspapers that I was involved with a bigamist. I would have died of embarrassment. So, I called an agency and hired a wonderful man by the name of Roberto.

CHARLENE. What did he do?

JANE. I met Roberto, and told him how I had been deceived by Willard, who was just after my money. I explained to Roberto that I wanted him to persuade Willard to leave town at once and never contact me again. Roberto was a former body builder and won several contests. I loved to watch his muscles ripple under his shirt as he moved.

CHARLENE. It's funny how many men look just like my Billy.

JANE. Roberto asked me to accompany him several times when he went out to follow Willard. He said he wanted me to point Willard out to him, as he wanted to make very sure he had the right man before he called on him. Willard might wear a disguise or something, you see. I had to go out with Roberto quite a few times before we finally saw Willard. I didn't mind though, Roberto was so charming. And such a good dancer.

LOUISE. So, then Roberto beat him up?

JANE. Please, Louise. Roberto isn't a thug, like some of your associates. It's true, Roberto wanted to take care of Willard right then and there, but I persuaded him to wait. I thought I should think about exactly what I wanted him to do.

LOUISE. What's to think about? Beat him up and send him on his way!

BETTY. Be quiet, Louise, and let her tell it her way.

JANE. So, the next evening I asked Roberto to take me dancing. He's so light on his feet, and of course, I think better on my feet. Roberto told me not to worry my pretty head about Willard, that he'd convince him to leave town quietly.

CHARLENE. Isn't that interesting. Billy had to go out of town on a business trip. Wouldn't that be funny if they both went to the same city?

BETTY. You just don't get it, do you? You're hopeless.

JANE. A few days later Roberto dropped by. He used the key I gave him, and found me resting by the pool. He told me he'd had a nice little "visit" with Willard and assured me everything was taken care of.

ROSEANN. Well, then, that's the end of that!

JANE. Well, uh, not quite. It seems Willard and Roberto discovered they had a lot in common, and they became… friends.

CHARLENE. I don't understand. What interest did they have in common?

JANE. Me! Look, everyone! *(shows engagement ring on her finger)* Roberto and I are engaged! And when we get married, Willard's going to be the best man. I know it's a bit unusual, but Roberto convinced me it's better to forgive and forget. Apparently, Roberto and Willard have some other past experiences in common also, and are planning on forming a partnership in some financial business. Try not to be jealous of my good fortune, girls.

WAITRESS. *(enters, serves desert)* Our specialty of the house, lemon puff pastries. I think. Or is it banana cream? They all look alike to me.

(sticks her finger in one and licks it)

No, it's lemon alright.

JANE. How disgusting. None for me, thanks.

ROSEANN. Well, I for one, am just delighted for you, honey! Roberto is right. It would have been better for me to forgive and forget too.

LOUISE. What do you mean? Don't tell me you went soft on the guy again!

ROSEANN. Oh, no. I followed through on my plan to get revenge alright. Remember, I said I was going to call my brother in Atlanta who is an IRS agent. He always said he'd take care of his little sister – that's me! So I called my brother, Charles, and he was outraged when he heard how that swindler had broken my heart. He wanted to challenge him to a duel, that's what gentle-men did in the old South, you know.

BARBARA. Do they still do that? I think that's illegal now.

ROSEANN. Well, Charles is old fashioned and a bit on the dramatic side. He belongs to a Civil war re-enactment group and loves to wear those tight pants and bran-dish a sword.

BETTY. Good grief! Don't tell me they had a sword fight!

ROSEANN. Of course not! Do you think we're that stupid? I wouldn't let Charles protect my honor in that manner. He might rip those tight pants! I had a better plan.

JANE. Get on with your story. I haven't got all day! I'm meeting Roberto shortly to discuss annuities.

ROSEANN. I explained to Charles that I wanted him to con-duct an audit on Wilson's tax records, find some tax evasions, and send him to jail!

LOUISE. That should take care of the dirty rat.

ROSEANN. I thought so, too, but there was a problem. You see, Charles couldn't do it himself, he was way too busy auditing some rich man in New York who owns a lot of property and businesses. They want to trump him! The IRS is very suspicious of him because he keeps firing people. So Charles turned my case over to his associate, Farley.

JANE. Never mind all the details. Just tell us the final outcome.

ROSEANN. That's what I'm getting to. Farley took over, and did a thorough investigation. He went over tax reports from the last ten years with a fine tooth comb, and found many, many " irregularities", as he put it. Farley said they could result in a long prison term, if they couldn't be explained properly in court.

JANE. That's great! Good for you, Roseann.

(All nod and express agreement.)

*(**ROSEANN** begins to cry.)*

BETTY. What's the matter, Roseann. Why are you crying? Aren't you happy Farley did such a good job?

ROSEANN. Farley did a good job alright. Only he got confused on what case he was supposed to investigate. He audited *my* tax records instead of Wilson's. *I appear in court next week!*

JANE. *(rises, goes to **ROSEANN** to comfort her)* You poor thing! What about you, Betty? We all left our last meeting with plans of revenge, and you remained at the table holding that picture of the man who was engaged to all of us. What did you do after we left?

LOUISE. Yeah, and as I remember, you had a very smug look on your face!

BETTY. Of course, I was as stunned as the rest of you. Although, I must confess that for a moment – just a fleeting second or two – the thought did cross my mind that with all of you out of the picture, I'd have Bill all to myself.

(*JANE returns to seat.*)

ROSEANN. Why would you want a scheming liar like that anyway?

BETTY. All of you were so angry, and were planning such terrible things to do to him, I couldn't help but feel sorry for him. I know you think I'm just a hard hearted attorney, but under this stern exterior beats a compassionate, forgiving nature. After all, I had truly fallen in love with Bill, and I couldn't forget all those tender moments we had – on Saturdays.

CHARLENE. I understand completely.

BETTY. We don't know what agony the poor man must have gone through, trying to keep all our dates straight. Hiding behind false pretenses, making excuses for his whereabouts. He must have felt some guilt, a twinge of remorse. We don't know what kind of dysfunctional family he came from – his father might have been married ten times and set a bad example for his son.

BARBARA. And so he was afraid of marriage, but enjoyed being engaged.

BETTY. Yes. He's a victim of that terrible addiction, A.D.D.D.

LOUISE. A.D.D.D?

BETTY. Any Dame'll Do Disease. There's a 12 step rehab program for it, and I'm sure I can get Bill enrolled in it, even though there is a long waiting list.
(*takes out picture*) I forgive you, Bill, darling. I'm the only one who truly understands you, and I'll be waiting for you. You're my one true love, and I'm sure after a little counseling, I'll be your one and only, too. You'll see. You'll all see!

WAITRESS. (*Enters, starts to clear dishes. Notices picture*) Hey! What are you doing with a picture of *MY HUSBAND?*

(*fast curtain*)

The End

COSTUME PLOT

BETTY – A business suit such as a retired professional might wear. She should have a hat with a very large red feather(s) appropriate to her title of the Prime Plume of the Red Feather Ladies Investment Club. Carries a briefcase with 8X10 picture of a man.

LOUISE – Loud, brightly colored mini dress or tight fitting capris and top. She wears a red feathered boa and lots of jewelry.

CHARLENE – Plain, neutral colored outfit. She has a large red feather pinned to her lapel. She wears glasses, and carries a purse, books, note pads, etc.

BARBARA – Layers of sweaters, scarves, hat with red feather. Plain walking shoes. Carries a large purse full of pill bottles and a fan. May use a cane or walker.

JANE – Attractive, expensive looking dress, suit or pant suit. Large pieces of jewelry to denote wealth. Wears a hat with red feathers, carries expensive looking purse.

ROSEANN – A summery, frilly dress, with lots of lace and ruffles, floppy sun hat with red feather attached.

WAITRESS – Typical waitress outfit, with tea apron. Carries an order pad, pencil and card from which she reads her greeting.

SET PLOT

Interior scene of Fancy Frills Tea Room.
Kitchen is stage left.
Outside door is stage right.
Set and walls are decorated with floral arrangements, vintage collectables, candles, teapots, etc.

PROPERTY PLOT PRESET

(Center)
Long table with 6 chairs, four facing audience and one at each end.
Tablecloth
Table settings for six (plates, silverware, cups, napkins, etc.)
Creamer and sugar
Jam, lemon curd for scones

(Stage left)
Small ice cream table and chairs, set for tea
Door to kitchen

(Stage right)
Easel holding poster with name "Fancy Frills Tea Room"
Outside door

(Offstage kitchen)
Water pitcher
Water glasses
Ice
Serving plate and scones
Serving plates and tea sandwiches
Serving plates and lemon pastries
Teapot
Large tray or serving cart

Also by
Maxine Holmgren...

Murder at the Grey's
Hound Mansion

Revenge of the
Red Feather Ladies

Who Shot Calhoun Cahootz?

9 780874 407341